Cunning Cat Tales

Cunning
Cat Tales

illustrated by Emma Chichester Clark

retold by Laura Cecil

Pavilion Children's Books

For Will
E.C.C.

For Isabel
L.C.

First published in Italy by Arnoldo Mondadori Editore S.p.A., in 2000
under the title *Il Gatto con gli Stivali e altre storie di gatti*

First published in Great Britain in 2001

This paperback edition first published in Great Britain in 2003 by
PAVILION CHILDREN'S BOOKS
64 Brewery Road
London N7 9NT

A member of **Chrysalis** Books plc

Text © Laura Cecil 2001
Illustrations © Emma Chichester Clark 2001
Design and layout © Pavilion Books Ltd.

The moral right of the author and illustrator
has been asserted

Designed by Bet Ayer

A CIP catalogue record for this book is available
from the British Library.

ISBN 1 84365 023 1

Set in Esprit Book

Printed and bound in Singapore by Kyodo

Colour origination by AGP Repro (UK) Ltd.

2 4 6 8 10 9 7 5 3 1

This book can be ordered direct from the publisher. Please contact
the Marketing Department. But try your bookshop first.

Contents

Introduction

"READ ME A STORY!" When I was little I used to interrupt my father with this cry. Luckily for me he usually gave in, and I can remember sitting on his knee, listening to the exploits of Puss in Boots and Jack the Giant-Killer. I was also happy to give in to this demand when my children did the same to me, as what could be nicer than sitting snuggled up together sharing a book?

This collection is designed particularly for reading aloud; it concentrates on direct speech rather than on description, giving opportunities for different voices and repeated phrases so that children can join in. In any case you only need to look at Emma's illustrations to see that Puss in Boots is clever, or that Bella's mother is bad-tempered. The distinctive type styles in the text help suggest sound effects, dramatic moments and different voices in order to add variety and expression to reading aloud. This also encourages young children beginning to read. All reading starts as reading aloud, and it is much easier to learn words and phrases if you can associate them with sounds and expressions.

About the Tales

Everyone knows *Puss in Boots*, but the other two stories in this collection are less familiar. *The White Cat* is a seventeenth-century French fairy tale by Madame d'Aulnoy, and *Sir Pussycat* is an Italian folktale (*Il Gatto Mammone*) similar to the better-known *Diamonds and Toads* by Perrault.

Puss in Boots

THERE WAS ONCE a miller who owned **a mill**, **a DONKEY** and **a cat**. When he died he left the mill to his oldest son, the donkey to his second son and **the cat** to the youngest son.

The two elder brothers went on with their father's work. But the youngest brother didn't know *what* to do. He could not understand how his father expected him to make a living with just **a cat**.

"I'd understand if he had left me a cow or some hens. Then at least I could have milk or eggs," he said miserably. "But **a cat! What use is a cat?** I suppose I could eat him and make a collar for my coat out of his fur…"

"Meow! Meow! You won't get much out of eating me or turning me into a collar!" said the cat. "I'm only skin and bone. Believe me, I'll be much more use to you alive than dead!"

"You'll have to be quick, Puss," said the young man. "My money has almost run out and if I don't find work soon, I'll have nothing to eat."

"Stop complaining!" snorted Puss. "Find me **a bag** and **a fine pair of boots.** Before a month is up, you'll understand how very lucky you were to inherit me. I am worth much more than **a DONKEY** and **a mill**, I can tell you!"

The miller's son didn't believe him, but he decided to humour Puss. He got him **a bag** and **a fine pair of boots.** **"Purr-fect!"** said the cat, as he pulled them on.

"With these I can work miracles." Then he set off for the woods with the bag over his shoulder.

13

When he came to the woods, he found a rabbit hole. He crept quietly, quietly until he was just outside it. First he opened the bag and put a carrot inside. Then he put the bag on the ground and lay down and pretended to sleep.

A few minutes later a pair of rabbits smelt the carrot and crawled into the bag.

QUICK AS A FLASH, Puss sprang up and trapped them inside. Then he set off for the royal palace feeling very pleased with himself.

At the palace gates Puss asked the soldiers to take him to the king.

"My master, *the Marquess of Carabas,* would like me to give you these two rabbits," said Puss bowing low. The king was delighted with the gift.

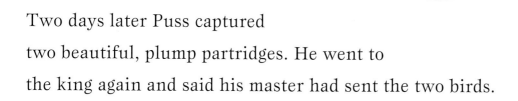

Two days later Puss captured two beautiful, plump partridges. He went to the king again and said his master had sent the two birds.

For the next month Puss visited the palace every other day. Each time he brought a gift for the king from the *Marquess of Carabas.*

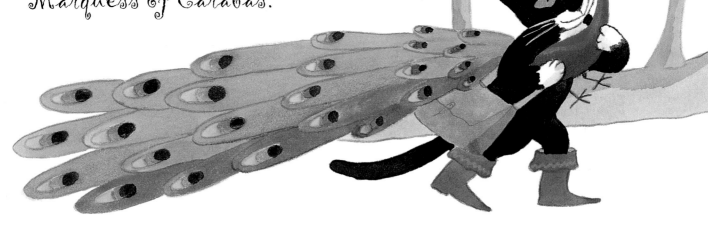

The king became very curious about the mysterious marquess, and asked to meet him. But Puss did not want the king to see his master in ragged clothes. So he thought up a plan.

One day he saw his chance when the king announced he was going for a drive with his daughter along the banks of the river.

16

Puss dashed back to his master's cottage and made him come to the river. **"Hurry! Get undressed and dive in,"** he said. "Soon the king's carriage will pass by.

Pretend you've had your clothes stolen while bathing, and say your name is the *Marquess of Carabas!*"

The young man did just as Puss told him. He got undressed, dived in the river and began to shout, **"HELP! HELP! Stop thief!** I'm the *Marquess of Carabas* and I've been robbed!"

Meanwhile Puss hid his master's ragged clothes. Then he ran in front of the king's carriage.

The king stopped the carriage immediately and ordered the guards to go and help.

Meanwhile Puss told the king how, when his master was bathing, a band of robbers, armed to the teeth, had seized his clothes, his horse and his money.

"Wicked, cruel men, your Majesty!"
Puss said in a trembling voice. "I was afraid
that they would kill my master. And now he is
almost naked, Majesty! They haven't even left him a cloak!"

"Don't worry, dear friend," said
the king. "My guards will go to the
palace to get some of my clothes
for the marquess. It is the least I
can do to repay the man who has
been so generous to me."

19

When the young man had put on the clothes, he went to meet the king and his daughter.

The miller's son was **transformed** by the beautiful clothes and he made a great impression on the princess. The king invited the marquess and his cat to spend several days at the palace.

20

"Unfortunately I have to deal with some urgent business for my master," said Puss. "But I am sure the marquess will be delighted to stay."

"Very delighted, indeed!" said the young man looking at the princess. He was already falling in love with her.

Meanwhile Puss was carrying on with his plan to make the king believe the miller's son was a real marquess. This time he needed to find a **splendid castle** for his master.

So while the carriage went back to the palace, he went the opposite way towards the estate of *Ogre Crunchbones.*

Puss crossed the ogre's fields and said to the peasants working on the land, "This land no longer belongs to *Ogre Crunchbones*. From today it belongs to the *Marquess of Carabas*. Very soon, the king will make a visit, and you must say that this is the marquess's land – or else you'll be cut into little pieces! Understand?"

The terrified peasants learnt the name of the *Marquess of Carabas* at once.

Then Puss went to the
ogre's castle. He knocked
at the door, and the ogre
himself opened it.

BOOM, BOOM, BOOM

Crunchbones was
hideous. He had
enormous gums
and pointed teeth,
a squashed nose
and eyebrows seven
times more thick
and hairy than
a man's.

"WHAT DO YOU WANT?"

he asked the cat menacingly.

"I had to walk past your castle," answered Puss,

"so I've come to pay you my respects."

This was most unusual. No one ever visited the ogre because he was

so horrible. So just to pass the time, he decided to let Puss in. "If I get

bored I can always eat him," thought the ogre.

"I have heard a lot about you and your magic," said Puss. **"But what they say sounds impossible."**

"And what do they say?" grunted the ogre as he picked his teeth.

"Oh, a lot of absurd nonsense," said Puss. "They say you can transform yourself into **a wild beast**."

"By a thousand broken bones, they are right!"

thundered the ogre, pounding his great hand on the table.
And he changed himself into **a lion** that opened its jaws
with a ferocious roar.

"Not bad!" said Puss coolly, hiding his fear.

"But that's easy for you. You are big and **a lion** is big! It would be different if you changed into a tiny animal. What about ... **a mouse**? That would be a real transformation!"

"I'll show you!"
roared the ogre.

A moment later there was
a mouse on the chair instead of
the ogre. QUICK AS A FLASH,
Puss swallowed it. Then he gave a
Cheshire Cat grin of triumph.

Next day he went back to the palace and told his master to take the king and the princess on a visit to his estate and his castle.

As the royal carriage passed by, the peasants did as Puss had told them. They waved their hats and shouted, "Welcome to the land of the *Marquess of Carabas*!" They were happy the ogre was dead.

The king already wanted the young man to marry his daughter and he was delighted to find that he was so rich.

Then Puss took them to the ogre's castle. "Marquess!" exclaimed the king, admiring the richly furnished rooms, "You are indeed a **lucky man!**"

Then the miller's son felt brave enough
to ask for the hand of the princess.
The king was very happy to say yes,
and in less than a month the two
young people were married.

Puss came to live at the
castle with his master and,
as he was a cat, he had
not **one** but **nine**
lives as a great lord.

The White Cat

O NCE UPON A TIME there was a king with **three sons**. They were all as handsome and brave as each other.

The king could not make
up his mind which one
should inherit his throne.
So he decided to set
them a test.
**"My sons, I will soon
be too old to rule,"**
he said.

"One of you will have to take my place. Whichever of you brings me the
most charming and faithful dog will become king. You have a year to find it."

Then he gave his sons enough money for their travels and said goodbye.

"*I will go north,*" said the first brother, and off he galloped on his white steed.

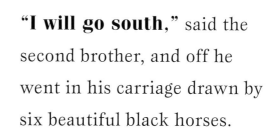

"**I will go south**," said the second brother, and off he went in his carriage drawn by six beautiful black horses.

"I will follow my nose," said the third prince, and off he set on foot towards the next kingdom.

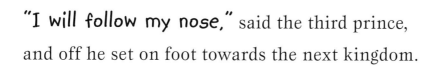

On the road he met every
kind of dog: big, little, black,
white, brown, long-eared,
curly-haired, spotty, shaggy,
short-haired, long-legged,
sausage-shaped…

"But how can I tell which will be the
most charming? And which will be
the **most faithful**?"
the prince wondered.

Day after day he wandered fruitlessly from kingdom
to kingdom looking for a dog to give his father.

One evening he was getting soaked in the rain
when he saw a castle high up on a hill.
"I will go there and seek shelter for
the night," he said. But when he got there
he was **dumbfounded**: the main door
was encrusted with precious
stones; the walls were crystal;
and the windows had gold
embroidered curtains.

The young man
knocked on the door
and a moment later he found
himself inside a splendid hall.

He couldn't see anyone except a dozen
gloved hands circling round him in the air.
They pushed him into a room, took off his
drenched clothes, washed him, dried him
and sprayed him with perfume. Then they
dressed him in fine clothes and took him to
a banqueting hall.

A beautiful white cat was sitting there at the head of the table. *"Welcome to my castle,"* she said. "Sit down beside me and have some food and drink."

"But … you can speak?" asked the young man, amazed.

"It's a long story," answered the cat, with a sad sigh. "But I won't bore you with it. Tell me about yourself instead. I know you are a prince, but what are you doing travelling in this storm?"

"Well, you see…" the prince began, and he told her his story.

"I am sure I can help you," said the cat when he had finished. "But there is not much time left before the year runs out, so why not stay with me until you must return to your father?"

The prince was happy to agree.

The white cat was a charming host. She gave the prince everything he wanted. They spent all day together and in the evening she entertained him with music.

On the day he left the white cat gave him **an acorn**. "Open this when you have to present your dog to the king," she said.

"I am most grateful, dearest cat," replied the young man. "If I hadn't promised to return to my father I would stay here. I have been so happy and I hope I will see you again."

41

When he returned to the palace, his brothers'
dogs were already sitting at the king's feet.
Then the prince took **the acorn** from
his pocket and opened it.

A tiny puppy jumped out
of the shell onto the
palm of his hand.

"I like all three dogs, especially the little one," said
the king. But he did not really want to give up his
throne, so he decided to set his sons another test:
"You have a year to find **a piece of linen so fine it
will go through the eye of a needle.**"

"*I will go north,*" said the first brother and off he galloped on his white steed.

"**I will go south,**" said the second brother and off he went in his carriage drawn by six beautiful black horses.

"I will follow my nose," said the youngest brother. But really he planned to go back to his friend, the white cat.

The cat was very happy to see him again. "I am sure I can find what your father wants," she said.

The year went by, and on the day the prince left she gave him **a walnut**. "I almost wish I were a cat…" exclaimed the young man as he said goodbye. "I have been so happy with you." Then he took the walnut and went back to his father's palace.

The king praised the fine cloth the two older brothers had brought. But he was amazed by what his youngest son pulled out of **the walnut** shell: **a piece of linen painted with the sea, the stars and the moon**. And it was so fine that it could pass through the eye of a needle.

Even so, the king still wanted to rule for another year.

"This will be your last test," he said. "Go and find a wife and bring her to the palace when the year is up. Whichever one of you finds **the most beautiful bride** will become king."

45

"I will go north," said the first brother and off he galloped on his white steed.

"I will go south," said the second brother and off he went in his carriage drawn by six beautiful black horses.

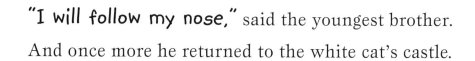

"I will follow my nose," said the youngest brother. And once more he returned to the white cat's castle.

"This time I have to bring my father **a beautiful bride**," explained the prince, when he greeted his friend. The cat was quiet for the rest of the day.

That evening she told the prince her story. *"I have not always been a cat,"* she began.

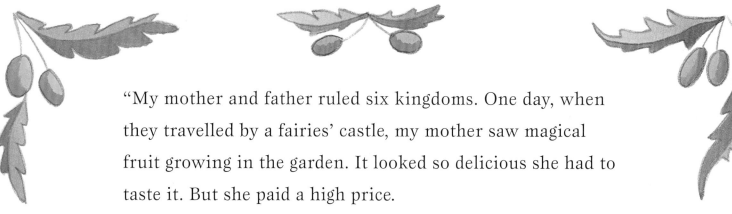

"My mother and father ruled six kingdoms. One day, when they travelled by a fairies' castle, my mother saw magical fruit growing in the garden. It looked so delicious she had to taste it. But she paid a high price.

"In return the fairies demanded her first-born child.

"So when I was born I was given to them and they carried me off to their castle. When I was eighteen they tried to make me marry a monster. He had the ears of a donkey, the legs of an eagle and a beard right down to the ground. But I said I would never be his bride.

"The monster flew away in a fury on his dragon. So, to punish me, the fairies turned me into a cat. The rest I cannot tell you…"

That evening the prince went to bed with a heavy heart. **If only he could free the princess from her enchantment.** She would be the perfect wife. She did not need to be beautiful. He did not care if he did not win his father's throne.

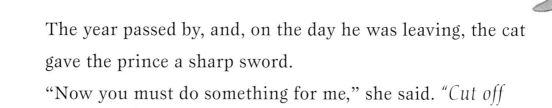

The year passed by, and, on the day he was leaving, the cat gave the prince a sharp sword.

"Now you must do something for me," she said. *"Cut off my head with this sword."*

"Never!" cried the young man, horrified. **"I could never hurt you!"**

"If you want to help me, and if you are my friend, *you must do it.* You and no one else…"

The prince tried not to listen, but the cat pleaded so hard that at last, with his eyes full of tears, he lifted the sword and cut off his friend's head.

Instantly, the body of the cat
began to change and moments later
a beautiful girl with eyes like stars
was standing before the prince.

At the same time the gloved hands
and the other cats in the castle were
also turned back into people.

"This is the end of the story," said the princess. "The fairies' spell could only be broken by a prince who loved me yet who would agree to kill me in my cat's body."

Then the prince asked her to be his bride. **The princess agreed at once.** They climbed into a golden coach and set off to see the prince's father.

When they arrived the young man got out of the coach and embraced his father. Then he opened the door of the coach and the princess stepped out.

53

She wore a magnificent dress. Her face,
her bearing and her voice enchanted
everyone there.

"You must be the one to take my place,"
said the king to his youngest son.

"May I speak, sire?" said the princess. "I think you should rule for many years to come. But I possess six kingdoms. We'll give one to you, one to your eldest son and one to your second son. That leaves three for us, which is quite enough!"

So everyone was happy: the king, the princes and their brides. They were all married on the same day and the splendid wedding party lasted all night.

Even the dogs danced!

Sir Pussycat

THERE WERE ONCE two little girls and, although they were sisters, they were quite different from each other. **Bertha** was lazy, ugly and spiteful, but *Bella* was pretty, patient and warm-hearted.

Even so, **Bertha** was her mother's favourite because she was just like her, and *Bella* was the one who was always punished.

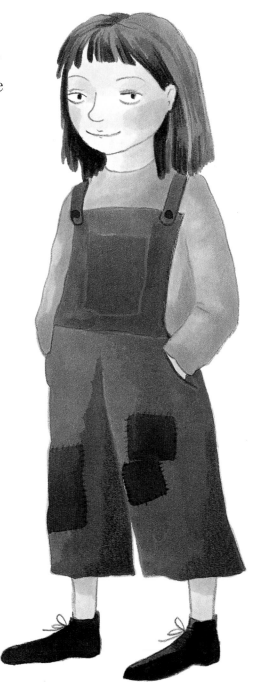

Time passed and the two little girls grew up. Even though *Bella* had to do all the washing, cooking and cleaning, she was always *cheerful* and *smiling*. But **Bertha** was always in a **bad mood**, even though she was never made to do anything.

One day Bella's mother told her to go to the stream and wash all the clothes. "Here's a bar of soap for you," she shouted. **"It's not cheap, so don't waste it!"**

When *Bella* reached the stream she tied her hair back
and began to sing as she soaped the washing.

Suddenly the soap slid out of her hand
down to the bottom of the stream.

Bella tried to get it back but the stream was too deep and the soap vanished. *"What shall I do?"* the poor girl wondered. "If I go back home with dirty washing and no soap, Mama will beat me!"

At the thought of her cruel mother, tears ran down her face.

At that moment, **a kind old lady** was passing by.
She saw *Bella* crying and stopped to ask what was the matter.

"I have to wash all these clothes," *Bella* explained, "but I've lost the soap in the stream. Mama will be furious with me. I'm afraid to go home and be beaten yet again."

"Don't you worry," said the old lady. "**I will show you how to find Sir Pussycat's house.** I am sure he will give you some soap."

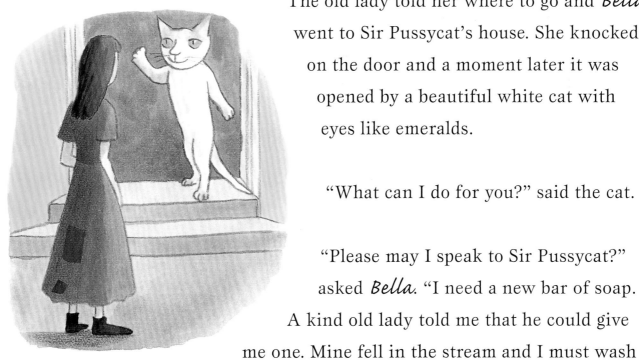

The old lady told her where to go and *Bella* went to Sir Pussycat's house. She knocked on the door and a moment later it was opened by a beautiful white cat with eyes like emeralds.

"What can I do for you?" said the cat.

"Please may I speak to Sir Pussycat?" asked *Bella*. "I need a new bar of soap. A kind old lady told me that he could give me one. Mine fell in the stream and I must wash a mountain of clothes by this evening, or there will be trouble at home…"

"All right, follow me," said the white cat, "I'll go and tell Sir Pussycat. As soon as he is free I will take you to him. Make yourself at home." Then the white cat disappeared down a long corridor.

Bella began to wander through the beautiful house. In one room she saw a little cat trying to sweep the floor with a broom almost twice his size.

"Let me do that for you," said *Bella*, and she took the broom and swept the whole floor.

When she had finished she went into another room. This time she saw a cat dusting. But in spite of his desperate leaps he was unable to reach the top of the tallest piece of furniture. *Bella* smiled, took the feather duster and dusted everywhere.

In the third room another cat was struggling to make the bed.

"If I help, we'll finish more quickly," said *Bella.* In less than no time she had made it.

At last the white cat came to say that Sir Pussycat was ready to receive her. Bella followed him to an even finer room than the others. There, sitting on an easy chair, was **Sir Pussycat**. He was enormous, with **long shiny fur** and the **kindest eyes** she had ever seen.

"Come here, Bella," said **Sir Pussycat**. "I know you have lost your soap and that you would like some more for your washing."

"I would be so grateful if you could give me some.
Mama would never forgive me if I lost ours."
Sir Pussycat sent for the cats whom
Bella had helped with
the housework.
He asked them if
Bella deserved a bar of soap.

"Oh yes!" said the first little
cat. "She helped me sweep the
whole floor!"

"Oh yes!" said the second little cat.
"She helped me dust everything in
the room!"

"Oh yes!" said the third little cat.
"She helped me make the bed."

"You've been a good girl," said **Sir Pussycat**. "Here is another bar of soap for you. Listen to me: when you go back to the stream, if you hear **a cockerel crowing** – turn around. But don't turn around if you hear **a donkey braying**!"

After this strange warning,
Sir Pussycat said goodbye.

Bella returned to the stream and began the washing. Suddenly she heard a **donkey braying** loudly. But she remembered **Sir Pussycat's** warning, and she did not turn round.

A few minutes later she heard **a cockerel crow**. She turned round and instantly **a golden star** appeared on her forehead. *Bella* finished her work and ran back home full of excitement.

As soon as her mother saw the **golden star** on her forehead, she was so envious that she forced *Bella* to tell her what had happened. Next day, she sent **Bertha** to the stream, so she could have a star just like her sister. **Bertha** made the soap slip into the water and started howling.

69

Just as before the **kind little old lady** passed by and advised **Bertha** to go to **Sir Pussycat** to ask for more soap.

Bertha went to the house and told her story to the white cat. He let her in and told her to wait.

She wandered sulkily into the first room and met the little cat with the big broom. But instead of helping she laughed at him. **"How ridiculous! A cat trying to use a broom!"**

Then she went into the second room and saw the cat dusting. "Would you be kind enough to help me dust high up where I cannot reach?" the cat asked her.

"Who do you take me for?" answered **Bertha** crossly. "I'm not your servant!"

Finally she came to the third room. "Could you help me straighten the sheet?" asked the cat. "It is hanging down too much on this side." **"Certainly!"** said **Bertha**. And she gave it such a tug that it undid all the bedclothes.

At that moment the white cat came and asked her to follow him.

When she was presented to **Sir Pussycat**, **Bertha** told her story
and demanded a bar of soap.

Then **Sir Pussycat** called the cats who did the housework and asked them if **Bertha** deserved to have the soap.

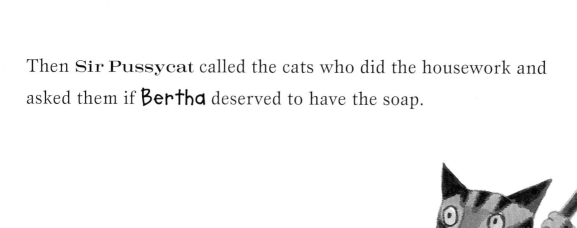

"Oh no!" said the first little cat. "She laughed instead of helping me!"

"Oh no!" said the second little cat. "She was rude instead of helping me!"

"Oh no!" said the third little cat. "She played a nasty trick instead of helping me!"

"Really?" said **Sir Pussycat**. "Nevertheless I will give you a bar of soap. Go back to the stream and wash the clothes. When you hear **a donkey braying**, turn round and look."

Bertha went to the stream and sat down to wait. As soon as she heard **a donkey braying**, she turned round ... and out of her forehead sprang **a donkey's tail!**

74

Her mother was beside herself with **rage** when she saw her favourite daughter. **"It's all her fault!"** said **Bertha**, pointing at her sister.

So her mother began to beat *Bella* until
she ran out of the house, crying.

At that moment, **the king's son was driving past** and heard her sobs. He stopped the carriage and went to see what was going on.

Bella told him everything and the prince took her away with him to the palace.

In no time at all he had fallen in love
with her, not just because of her **beauty**, but
because of her **goodness** and **cheerfulness**.

After a few days he asked her to marry him.
Bella was just as much in love, and said yes at once.

The prince wanted to punish her mother and sister severely, but *Bella* begged him to be merciful. She thought **Sir Pussycat** had punished **Bertha** and her mother enough.

So the prince ordered the two women to leave the country and **nobody ever saw them again**.

Bella and the prince's wedding
was magnificent.

It is strange that the Prince went past *Bella's* house just when she really needed him and it is very lucky that he did.

But perhaps **Sir Pussycat** had something to do with that as well!